G·FORCE

THE MOVIE STORYBOOK

Adapted by Sierra Harimann

Based on the screenplay by The Wibberleys and
Ted Elliott & Terry Rossio and Tim Firth

Based on a story by Hoyt Yeatman

Executive Producers Mike Stenson, Chad Oman,
Duncan Henderson, David James

Produced by Jerry Bruckheimer

Directed by Hoyt Yeatman

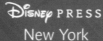

DISNEP PRESS

New York

Visit www.disneybooks.com

Visit www.disney.com/g-force

Printed in the United States of America

First edition

1 3 5 7 9 10 8 6 4 2

Library of Congress Catalog Card Number on file

ISBN 978-1-4231-1288-4

SUSTAINABLE FORESTRY INITIATIVE
Certified Chain of Custody
40% Certified Forests,
60% Certified Fiber Sourcing
www.sfiprogram.org
PWC-SFICOC-260

FOR TEXT PAPER ONLY

It was out of his hands. Scientist Ben Kendall had prepared his team. Now it was up to them. The mission: to infiltrate the home of Leonard Saber.

Saber was a rich businessman. He was the owner of Saberling Industries, maker of household appliances and of electronic hardware used by the U.S. military. For two years, the National Security Agency had been watching Saber. They believed he was developing technology to sell to the enemies of the United States and that this technology was referred to by the code name Clusterstorm. Tonight, Ben's agents—three guinea pigs, a fly, and a mole, all dressed from whisker to paw in spy gear—would have their one chance to expose Saber's plans. If they didn't succeed, it would be their first—and last—mission.

"Your mission," Ben told the team, "is to download the 'Clusterstorm' files from Saber's personal computer, located in his study." He paused before adding, "You've all been genetically engineered and specially trained for this moment. You can do it!"

Later that night, the team leader, Darwin, poked his head out from behind the branches of a tree on the edge of Saber's property. He leaped out of the tree and landed at its base. Within seconds, he was scanning the grounds using his night-vision goggles.

Meanwhile, Speckles, a virtually blind star-nosed mole, was stationed nearby in his mole hole. He was the communications point-rodent, and his meticulous attention to detail served the team well. After Darwin confirmed visual on Saber, Speckles checked in on the rest of the team. He confirmed that Juarez, a feisty Latina guinea pig, and Blaster, her gung-ho partner, had infiltrated the grounds via underwater and were now stationed on the mansion's roof preparing Darwin's exit. Finally he connected with Mooch, the surveillance housefly.

"Speckles to Mooch," he said. "Getting no visual. Over."

Suddenly Speckles's monitor came to life, showing the interior of the mansion through Mooch's tiny camera. Speckles watched as Saber addressed the crowd gathered in the ballroom.

"Welcome," Saber said gallantly. The crowd settled down and gave him their attention. "For years we've been putting a secret into the heart of every member of the Saberling family. Be it the new cryogenic refrigerator or the new microwave-heated coffeemaker."

On a screen behind Saber a logo appeared. It read: SABERSENSE. His voice growing more excited, Saber explained that in forty-eight hours he would press a button to activate the wireless SaberSense system. All the Saberling appliances would then be connected.

As Saber made his speech, the G-Force was hard at work. From the roof, Blaster and Juarez ran a cable down the inside of the chimney that rose from Saber's study.

Darwin had scampered into Saber's office, which was lit by the flames from Saber's electric fireplace. Clapping his paws twice, the flames died. Then Darwin raced across the desk and pulled out his personal digital assistant, placing it next to Saber's laptop. Punching away at the PDA keyboard, Darwin watched as information began to flash across the screen.

Meanwhile, in the ballroom, Saber had finished his speech and was headed upstairs. Darwin had five seconds. He worked furiously at the laptop. Suddenly a countdown clock appeared on the screen. It read: CLUSTERSTORM D-DAY T-MINUS 47:55:00.

"Speckles, are you seeing this?" Darwin asked.

"I see it," Speckles answered.

They were running out of time. Darwin hit a button and began downloading the files to his PDA. It seemed to take forever.

Finally the transfer was complete. Darwin disconnected the PDA and slipped it into his pocket. Quickly, he headed for the fireplace. He grabbed the cable just as Saber entered the study, clapping his hands twice.

Darwin was yanked up the chimney just as the fire ignited, and the flames singed his furry bottom.

"Whooooooooah!" Darwin shouted as he flew through the air, fur smoldering. "We got it!" he said when he landed on the roof. Racing to the edge of the roof, Darwin, Blaster, and Juarez jumped. Moments later their parachutes deployed and they landed safely.

Mission accomplished.

The next morning, at their headquarters, the team prepared for the arrival of the FBI. Ben and his assistant, Marcie, cleaned the area. In their individual living pods, the team worked out, researched, or relaxed. Finally, the agents arrived. Director Kip Killian was accompanied by Agents Trigstad and Carter. All three seemed very serious.

Ben introduced the team and then eagerly began to explain the usefulness of animal intelligence. Killian was not impressed. So Ben tried to show the director what his team could do. Walking over to Speckles, they saw the mole hard at work on his computer. Using the animal translator Ben had invented, the humans in the room heard Speckles say, "We're ready."

Turning to the three men, Ben told them about the Saber mission.

"You ran a mission without my authorization?" Killian asked, his face stern.

Ben gulped. "Sir, we knew we were up for review and wanted to show you what we could do."

Speckles opened the file Darwin had downloaded at Saber's. It showed . . . a coffeemaker. The G-Force looked at each other. This was *not* good.

Agent Killian beckoned Ben to follow him outside. "Kendall, this entire lab is an embarrassment," he scolded. "I'm shutting you down."

"Please don't do this," Ben pleaded.

"No!" Killian barked. "I'm not gonna take the heat for this." He turned to the other agents. "Dr. Kendall is coming with me."

Inside, watching through Mooch's spy camera, Marcie gasped. "They're arresting him!"

The team realized they needed to make a run for it if they didn't want to end up as lab rats. They used special air tunnels to evacuate. They shot out of the warehouse into the open and found themselves on an industrial loading dock.

But they weren't in the clear yet! Suddenly, Trigstad and Carter appeared on the dock. The G-Force was trapped! Darwin looked around desperately for an escape. Then he saw the answer—a pallet full of pet supplies was nearby. On top was a pet carrier!

"We can hide in here," Darwin cried. Dragging a reluctant Speckles, the team climbed inside the carrier. The door shut and locked behind them.

Sitting in silence, the G-Force heard Trigstad and Carter talking to someone outside the carrier. "Hey, facility is closed," Trigstad said. He was talking to the pet-store employee, Terrell, who had been unloading supplies. "Take your delivery back," Trigstad added. Shrugging, Terrell prepared to leave.

"We're locking the building down, Agent Killian," Trigstad then said into his cell phone. He paused. He didn't want to say what he was about to. "But the animals have all bolted," he added. There was silence while on the other end of the phone Killian shouted his orders. Trigstad and Carter were to get the animals back—dead or alive.

Terrell drove back to Elia's Pet Shop, where he worked. When he began to unload the truck he noticed his new passengers. Shrugging, he brought them inside and placed them in a big glass terrarium. Inside, the ground was covered in wood chips, and in the corner, a cute hamster stared at them. But when Darwin came closer, the hamster began jumping up and down. "Do *not* cross that line!" he yelled.

As the hamster was screaming, another resident of the cage came over. It was the fattest guinea pig the team had ever seen. His name was Hurley. After introducing himself, he made Bucky—the hamster—leave them alone.

The team wasted no time and began to look for a way out. Blaster ran straight at the glass sides and ended up knocking himself out. And when the other members tried to get out the top, they couldn't reach it. Things did not look good.

"So, Hurley," Darwin said, turning to the other guinea pig, "how do you get out of here?"

Hurley was shocked. "You guys don't want to stay in a place where food falls from the sky and you can poop wherever you like?"

The G-Force shook their collective heads.

"Only one way out," Hurley said. "Get adopted."

Just then, Mooch landed on the outside of their cage. Darwin told him to go find Ben. Mooch quickly buzzed off. Then, after Darwin explained to Hurley who they were and why it was so important that they leave, he made his next decision. Eyeing an older man and his grandchildren who had just entered the store, he said, "We get adopted, then we escape. Now go act cute!"

In the corner, Speckles sighed. He knew this was useless. Who would ever adopt an ugly blind mole?

"Come on," Darwin said, seeing the hopeless look on his teammate's face. "You too, Speckles."

A few moments later, Juarez and Blaster had been plucked from the cage and packed off to their new home. Before they left, Blaster promised to escape, find Ben, and return to rescue Darwin and Speckles.

"Specks, we have to think of a way out of here," Darwin said when they were alone.

The two remaining members of the G-Force quickly hatched a plan. Speckles would fake his death. The humans would bury him and then he could dig himself out. He'd wait until nightfall to sneak back into the pet store through the mail slot to set Darwin free. It was foolproof!

At first, the mission went according to plan. Speckles played dead and Terrell put him in a bag and headed for the back door. But before he could make it to the store's yard, a garbage truck pulled up.

Darwin watched in horror as Terrell tossed Speckles into the back of the truck. In moments, the mole had disappeared.

Later that night, Darwin sat in sad silence. He had failed as a leader and paid a heavy price—the loss of one of his team.

Hurley noticed his new friend's silence. He decided to cheer him up by showing him a picture—of cake. "This is why I live," he said. Hurley continued to rave about cake until he noticed something. He and Darwin had the same birthmark! But when he pointed this news out to Darwin, the leader just shrugged. He had more important things to think about—like getting out.

Meanwhile, back at his house, Ben was trying to find more on Saber's disk. But suddenly, his laptop crashed! The Saber software had infected it with an extermination virus! What was going on?

Back at the pet shop, Darwin had discovered a way out. Bucky had been covering up an escape hatch the entire time! Darwin didn't think twice. He said good-bye to his cagemates and escaped. But Bucky shoved Hurley out, too!

Hurley landed on the ground behind Darwin. They were forced to stay together. Darwin wasn't happy, but Hurley was excited—maybe he would find some of the cake he had always dreamed about.

Darwin knew he had to find the rest of his team, get to Ben, and stop Saber. But he also knew it was going to be a long journey. . . .

The next morning, back at his house, Ben received a surprise visit from Mooch. The fly quickly buzzed over to the computer keyboard and spelled out where the team was—Elia's! Ben hopped on his bike and headed out to save his friends.

What he didn't know was that Agents Trigstad and Carter were following him and now had a lead on G-Force's location.

Not too far away, Darwin and Hurley were hiding in some bushes. They were making their way to Ben's. But with Hurley along, it was slow going. Then, it got worse. Much worse.

"Dogs!" screamed Hurley, catching sight of lots of big—and hungry-looking—canines. They were going to be eaten alive!

Luckily, Darwin was trained to get out of hairy situations. Leaping into action, he pushed Hurley into an old tire. Soon they were rolling away from the danger and onto a main street.

When it was safe, they quickly abandoned the tire and walked down the street, looking into windows. Suddenly, Darwin came to a halt.

Inside an appliance store Darwin saw the same coffeemaker that had been on display at Saber's house.

Sneaking inside the store, Darwin began to disassemble the machine. He pulled out a microchip attached to the machine by a bunch of wires. Darwin noticed that the coffeemaker featured the same countdown clock he had seen at Saber's.

"Do you know what this is?" Darwin asked Hurley, holding up the chip.

"Uh, yeah," Hurley answered. "I'm pretty sure it's called vandalism."

"Military-grade, multiple-array transceiver," Darwin corrected. "Developed for the military's Unmanned Weapons Program."

Darwin was about to pull the chip out when the coffeemaker suddenly came to life and turned into a robot—complete with weapons! It locked its aim on Darwin, who ducked and rolled across the counter just in time to avoid being hit by a laser beam. Another beam shot out of the machine, burning a hole in the glass behind Hurley.

"Run!" Darwin yelled.

Together, the two guinea pigs jumped through the hole in the glass and fell to the ground outside. The coffeemaker followed.

"I don't think that thing makes decaf," Hurley observed.

Darwin ignored Hurley and turned to face the machine. He had to get that chip!

Using all his skills, he lured the machine into the street. A moment later, it was crushed by a passing truck. They were safe—for now.

"What is this thing?" Hurley asked.

"Saber's weaponizing his entire line of appliances," Darwin answered.

They *had* to get to Ben's—fast.

While Darwin and Hurley were facing off against a killer coffee machine, Blaster and Juarez were facing something much, much scarier—their new owners, Conner and Penny.

Inside Penny's room, Juarez found herself dressed in doll's clothes. She even had on earrings and lipstick. She was about to show Penny just how skilled a martial artist she was when Blaster came to the rescue.

Unlike Juarez, Blaster had been having fun with Conner. Conner let him play in machine cars and race around. But Blaster knew they had to get out. When Conner wasn't looking, Blaster took control of the remote-controlled car he was in. Racing out of the house, he rescued Juarez.

Noticing his teammate's new look, he almost said something. But Juarez's expression stopped him cold. Instead, he turned the car in the direction of Ben's and headed out.

Soon, the whole team—minus Speckles—was reunited. When Ben heard about Speckles, he was devastated. He thought it was his fault. He had lied to his team—they hadn't been genetically engineered. They were ordinary rodents who had been specially trained.

Juarez had been rescued from a taco restaurant.

Blaster came from a cosmetics company.

Speckles had been taken from a golf course. And Darwin? He had come from a pet store.

After Ben made his confession, the G-Force was silent for a moment. Then, Darwin stood up.

"We may be guinea pigs, but we're not ordinary," he said, his voice full of bravery. "I still believe in us!"

The team was back! Now it was time to take down Saber. And they only had thirty minutes!

The G-Force needed a plan. When Ben told them about the virus that had destroyed his computer, they had it. They would use the virus to destroy Saber's system.

There was no time to lose. Ben introduced the team to his RDV— Rapid Deployment Vehicle. It was made up of three clear hamster balls that were attached but could separate if needed. It was go time!

Unfortunately, Agents Carter and Trigstad were close behind. As the G-Force drove through the streets, the agents struggled to stay on their trail. But it wasn't easy.

High in the sky, Mooch relayed shortcuts to his team. When they raced through a fireworks display, it was over. The agents got caught in the explosion while the G-Force drove on toward Saber's.

Saber, meanwhile, was unaware that the G-Force was closing in. He was seated at a desk inside his study. A Saberling 5000 coffeemaker sat in front of him, and six video monitors showing the faces of his executive team glowed on the opposite wall. One screen—labeled "Mr. Yanshu: China"—was blank.

"Our time has finally arrived," Saber announced. "SaberSense technology ushers in the dawn of a new age. . . ."

As he spoke, the G-Force infiltrated the mansion's ventilation system. Leaving Hurley to keep their exit safe, the three others slipped down a chute that would lead them to the core of Saberling.

But when they got there, they found it was booby-trapped!

Upstairs, Saber pushed a button on the coffee machine. . . .

Suddenly, all across the country, Saberling appliances began to attack the people who owned them. Garbage disposals went after moms in their kitchens. Refrigerators pelted children with ice cubes. Lawn mowers chased dads around their yards. Even Saber was being attacked!

Agent Killian and his team arrived at Saber's mansion expecting to find the businessman enjoying the launch of his deadly program. They were shocked to instead find Saber and his assistant cowering in a corner on the second floor of the mansion, terrified.

Killian and his team grabbed the pair and, dodging the machines, raced outside to the relative safety of their observation truck.

Down in the basement, the G-Force was trying to make their way through the booby traps to the computer core so that they could shut it down.

Suddenly, they heard an odd whirring noise. Turning, their eyes grew wide.

Hurley was trapped—inside a microwave oven. And the machine was about to select a cooking time!

Wasting no time, Darwin rushed over to Hurley and tried to free him. Inside, Hurley was panicking and kept looking anxiously back . . . at a piece of cake!

Just as the microwave pinged on, Darwin grabbed a cord hanging from the ceiling and swung himself toward the door. With a click, the door opened up, releasing Hurley.

Hurley's close encounter was too much. Darwin couldn't risk the rest of his team. He had no choice. He was going into the core—alone.

Inside the command truck, Killian had handcuffed Saber to a chair and was questioning him.

"I find it pretty hard to believe that you've got nothing to do with this," Killian said roughly. At that moment, a tech came in and mentioned the word Clusterstorm.

"Yanshu came up with that word," Saber said. "He runs manufacturing. I've got *nothing* to do with manufacturing!"

As Saber claimed his innocence, Ben and Marcie arrived. They had tracked the team to the mansion. Suddenly, Mooch's video feed popped up on Ben's handheld system. It revealed an image of Darwin.

"He's going to insert a virus into the core and take down the network," Ben explained. He looked at Killian. "*If* we have authority."

Killian barely hesitated. He gave the go-ahead.

In the basement, Darwin finally arrived at the computer core.

"Hello, Darwin," a voice said.

Darwin froze. It was Speckles!

Speckles revealed that he had been disguising himself as Yanshu—which was the Chinese word for mole—and working with Saber for years. It had all been part of his plan.

From the command truck, Saber, Ben, Marcie, and Killian watched in disbelief.

"Yanshu was in my basement the whole time?" Saber asked.

"And he wasn't a man, he was a mole," Ben said. He shook his head. How could Speckles have betrayed them?

In the basement, Darwin kept talking to Speckles. "You infected my PDA. You sabotaged our presentation," he said. "Why?"

"Extermination virus. Nasty stuff," Speckles admitted. "Ever Googled the word 'mole'? Three million entries on how to exterminate them. Not for trivial reasons, of course. For real important reasons, like *golf courses*!"

Speckles buckled himself into his chair. Suddenly, the ground began to shake. From all around the house, appliances were coming together to form Clusterstorm—a giant robot. An arm reached out from the massive machine and plucked up Speckles and his computer console, placing them on top so that Speckles became the head.

Darwin jumped onto the Clusterstorm beast as it rose up and out of the house. Below, the rest of the team grabbed on to dangling cables and tried to make their way to Darwin. He was just about to connect the infected PDA when it slipped from his grasp.

Observing the chaos below him, Speckles smiled. His plan was working. His dream of making humans feel small and helpless was coming true!

But it was not to be. With Mooch's help, Darwin got back the PDA. He slammed it into the computer dock. In seconds, the huge structure began to crumble. The G-Force jumped to safety, parachuting to the ground. Soon, Clusterstorm was nothing but broken machines.

Mission: Accomplished.

A few weeks later, the G-Force was finally relaxing. Hurley, the newest member of the team, was barbecuing when Marcie came in with a new recruit—Bucky!

G-Force was official. They had the badges and now they also had the recruits. They were ready for whatever mission—big or small—came next.